Mommy's Treasure

Written by
Widline Angel Pyrame

Illustrated by
Zoya Khan

Fusion Dolls Publishing

Dedication

This book is dedicated to every
child who was prayed for, hoped for,
and lovingly welcomed into the world.

And to my precious miracle baby, Zurie—
I love you more than words can ever say.
You will always and forever be Mommy's treasure.

Fusion Dolls Publishing

Mommy's Treasure

by Widline Angel Pyrame,

COPYRIGHT

Written by: Widline Angel Pyrame
Illustrated by: Zoya Khan
Published by: Fusion Dolls Publishing
First Edition: 2026
Printed in the United States of America

I prayed for you. I wished for you.
And then ... you were here.

My heart is full of love for you...

I love you bigger than the sky.

I love you deeper than the sea.

My love will never, ever end.

I love reading with you.
Your eyes shine so bright!

I love walking with you.
You find new things to see!

You are Mommy's treasure...

Your smile is magic.
Your eyes smile, too...

Everyone loves your happy face.

The moon is in the sky.
It's time for bed, my sweet.

Bath Time

First, a warm bath.
Splash, splash, splash!
We brush your little teeth.
Brush, brush, brush!

"I wrap you in a soft, warm towel..."

I sing your favorite song...

Now you are clean and cozy...

Which one will we read?
Daddy's Little Girl!

You smile at the pictures.
I smile, too.

Peace like a river...

Daddy gives you a goodnight kiss...

"muh-muh-muh"

I pick you up. You laugh.
I laugh, too.
You are Mommy's treasure.
I will always protect you.
I will always love you.
If you ever feel sad,
remember this is true:
Mommy loves you,
always and forever.
I prayed for you,
I waited for you.
And now... you are here.
You are my treasure.
My love will be
with you, always
and forever.

About the Author

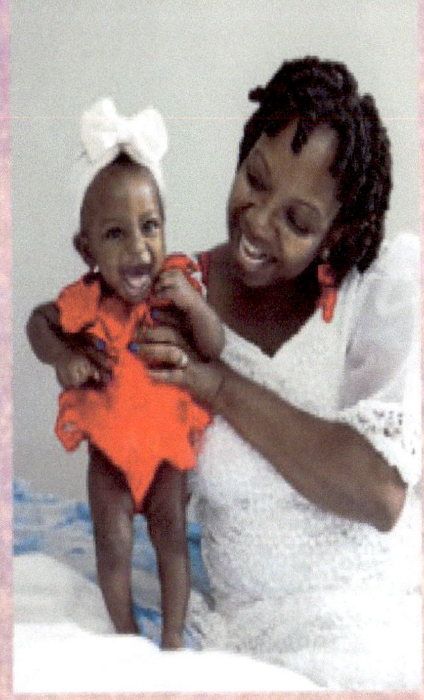

Widline Angel Pyrame is a Haitian-American author, entrepreneur, and licensed social worker. She is also the founder of Fusion Dolls, a brand created to celebrate representation, confidence, and the beauty within every child.

This story was inspired by her daughter, **Zurie**, whose joy and presence continue to guide Widline's creative journey.

Through her books, Widline hopes to uplift families, honor cultural pride, and remind every little one that they are loved, valued, and wonderfully made.